THE DOG COOKIE

BY MICHÈLE DUFRESNE

CONTENTS

Pioneer Valley Educational Press, Inc.

chapter one
JACK AND DAISY ARGUE

Daisy walked outside.
Jack was lying down on a rock
in the sun.

Daisy went over to Jack.
"Do you want to play ball?"

"Yes!" said Jack.
"That sounds like fun!"

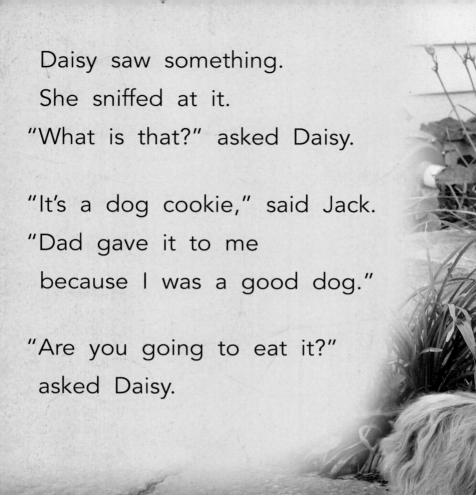

Daisy saw something.
She sniffed at it.
"What is that?" asked Daisy.

"It's a dog cookie," said Jack.
"Dad gave it to me
    because I was a good dog."

"Are you going to eat it?"
asked Daisy.

5

"No," said Jack.
"I don't like how it smells.
 I don't think I like dog cookies."

 Daisy sniffed again.
"I think it smells yummy!"
 she told Jack.
"Can I have it?"

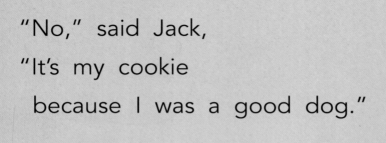

"No," said Jack,
"It's my cookie
 because I was a good dog."

"I'm a good dog," said Daisy.
"Please give it to me.
 I love dog cookies!"

"I want to keep it," said Jack.
"Dad gave it to me."

"Please, please give it to me!
You don't want the cookie
and I do," said Daisy.

"No," said Jack.
"I'm not giving you my cookie."

"That's so mean, Jack!" shouted Daisy.
"I'm not going to play ball with you.
I'm going to go play by myself."
She stomped off.

Jack started to cry.
"I am not mean,"
he said.
"It's my cookie.
  Dad gave it to me."

chapter two

ROSIE HELPS OUT

Rosie went to the door
and looked out.
"Why are you crying, Jack?"

Jack sniffed.
"Daisy shouted at me.
She won't play ball with me."

Rosie went over to Jack.
"Oh dear," said Rosie.
"Why did Daisy shout
at you and why won't she play
ball with you?"

Jack showed Rosie his dog cookie.
"Daisy wants the cookie Dad gave
to me," he told Rosie.

Rosie sniffed the cookie.
"It smells yummy.
Are you going to eat it?"
she asked.

"I don't think it smells good,"
said Jack. "I don't like dog cookies."

"Oh," said Rosie.
"I think it smells good.
  Can I eat it?"

"I want to keep it," said Jack.
"Dad gave it to me
  because I was a good dog."

"Oh," said Rosie.
"I think I have an idea."

"Let's break the cookie
   into three pieces,"
   said Rosie.
"You can keep
   a piece of the cookie,
   I can eat a piece,
   and Daisy can eat a piece,"
   she told Jack.

Jack liked this idea.
"OK," he said.

"Daisy," called Jack,
"Come and get a piece of my cookie!"

"Thank you, Jack," said Daisy.
"Now let's go play ball!"